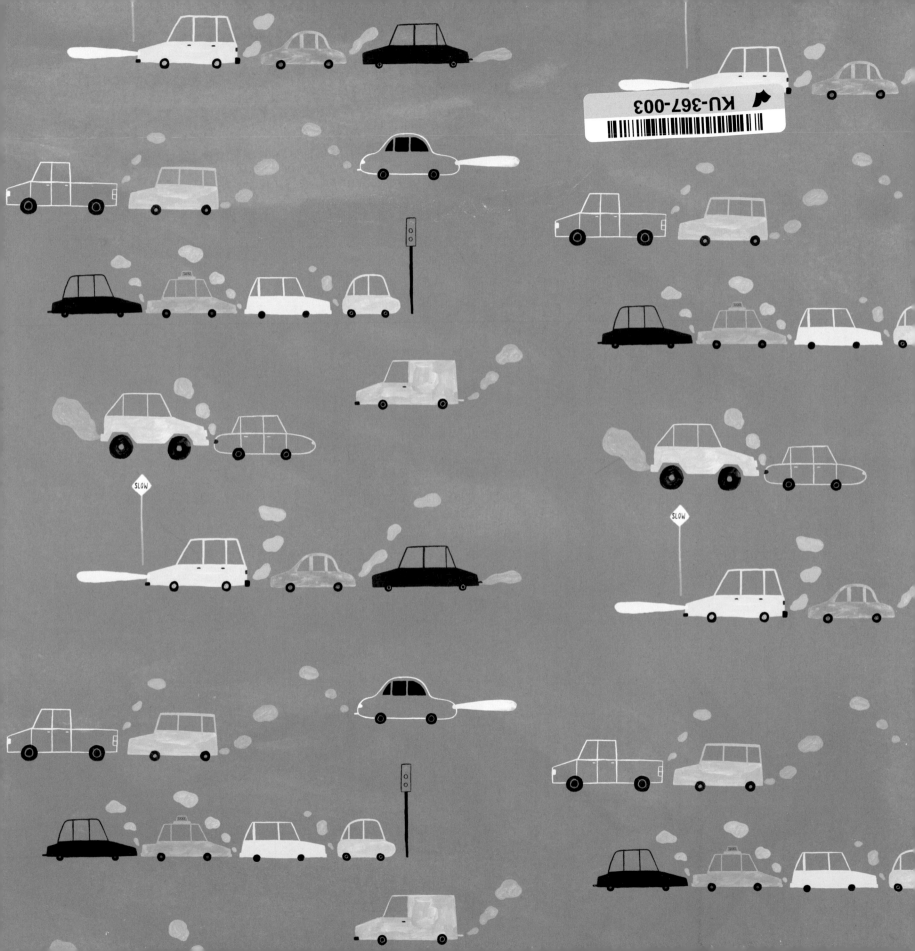

For my grands and great niblings

Naomi

First published in 2021 by Child's Play (International) Ltd
Ashworth Road, Bridgemead, Swindon SN5 7YD, UK

Published in USA in 2021 by Child's Play Inc
250 Minot Avenue, Auburn, Maine 04210

Distributed in Australia by Child's Play Australia Pty Ltd
Unit 10/20 Narabang Way, Belrose, Sydney, NSW 2085

Text copyright © 2021 Naomi Danis
Illustrations copyright © 2021 Child's Play (International) Ltd
The moral rights of the author and illustrator have been asserted

ISBN 978-1-78628-566-9
SJ260221CPL04215669

Printed and bound in Shenzhen, China

1 3 5 7 9 10 8 6 4 2

A catalogue record of this book
is available from the British Library

www.childs-play.com

BYE, CAR

Naomi Danis

illustrated by Daniel Rieley

Bye, car.

Bye, another car.

Bye, near car.

Bye, far car.

Bye, grown-up car.

Bye, baby car.

Bye, big car.

Bye, tiny car.

Bye, red car.

Bye, blue car.

Bye,
vroom-vroom-vroom
car.

Bye,
zooming car.

Bye, car in a hurry.

Bye, car in a flurry.

Bye, howling car.

Bye, growling car.

Bye, noisy car.

Bye, quiet car.

Bye, car driving slow.

Bye, car honking go.

Bye,
winking car.

Bye,
blinking car.

Hello, new day.

Hello, bus.

Hi, bicycles passing us.

Hello, tram.
Here I am!

Hello, vehicles
greener, cleaner.

Hello!

ECO
RIDE